Shai & Emmie

STAR IN

TO THE RESCUE!

To Zorea, Sammie, and Shuga—my pets—
and all the animals that need love and a better home
—Q. W.

For Clara Hyacinth Ohlin
—N. E. O.

To my niece, Emma
—S. M.

SIMON & SCHUSTER BOOKS FOR YOUNG READERS
An imprint of Simon & Schuster Children's Publishing Division
1230 Avenue of the Americas, New York, New York 10020
For information about special discounts for bulk purchases, please contact
Simon & Schuster Special Sales at 1-866-506-1949 or business@simonandschuster.com.
The Simon & Schuster Speakers Bureau can bring authors to your live event. For more information or to book an event,
contact the Simon & Schuster Speakers Bureau at 1-866-248-3049 or visit our website at www.simonspeakers.com.
Book design by Chloë Foglia
The text for this book was set in Bembo.
The illustrations for this book were rendered in watercolor and ink.
Manufactured in the United States of America, 0518 FFG
First Edition
2 4 6 8 10 9 7 5 3 1
Library of Congress Cataloging-in-Publication Data
Names: Wallis, Quvenzhané, 2003– author. | Ohlin, Nancy, author. | Miller, Sharee (Illustrator), illustrator.
Title: Shai & Emmie star in To the rescue! / Quvenzhane Wallis with Nancy Ohlin ; illustrated by Sharee Miller.
Other titles: Shai and Emmie star in To the rescue! | To the rescue!
Description: First edition. | New York : Simon & Schuster Books for Young Readers, 2018. |
Series: A Shai & Emmie story | Summary: Third-grader Shai is already busy with her mother away and the Student
Orchestra's benefit concert coming up, but that does not stop her from helping a stray animal in her backyard.
Identifiers: LCCN 2017048132 (print) | LCCN 2017057922 (ebook) |
ISBN 9781481458887 (hardback) | ISBN 9781481458900 (ebook)
Subjects: | CYAC: Family life—Fiction. | Orchestra—Fiction. | Rabbits—Fiction. | Wildlife rescue—Fiction. |
Friendship—Fiction. | African Americans—Fiction. | BISAC: JUVENILE FICTION / Readers / Chapter Books. |
JUVENILE FICTION / Social Issues / Friendship. | JUVENILE FICTION / Social Issues / Adolescence.
Classification: LCC PZ7.1.W357 (ebook) | LCC PZ7.1.W357 Shn 2018 (print) | DDC [Fic]—dc23
LC record available at https://lccn.loc.gov/2017048132

Shai & Emmie

STAR IN

TO THE RESCUE!

Quvenzhané Wallis

WITH Nancy Ohlin   ILLUSTRATED BY Sharee Miller

Simon & Schuster Books for Young Readers

NEW YORK   LONDON   TORONTO   SYDNEY   NEW DELHI

Program

SCENE 1

G for "Goose"

Shai Williams positioned her fingers on the clarinet. Its name was Clara the Clarinet (although Shai had been thinking about changing the name to Sadie or maybe Kennedy). She closed her lips over the mouthpiece, tucked her chin, and made laser eyes at the conductor's baton. The other musicians in the orchestra were watching the baton too.

The conductor, Mr. Yee, scanned their faces. He nodded and smiled. Then he breathed in quickly and raised the baton. This meant: *Let's all get ready to play the first note!*

A second later he breathed out quickly and lowered the baton. This meant: *Time to* play *the first note!*

Shai blew into the mouthpiece eagerly. Her first note was a G. Or it was *supposed* to be a G,

anyway. It sounded more like a goose honking.

G for "Goose," she thought unhappily. *G for "I Goofed Gigantically."* She tried to adjust the

note with her breath, but the harder she tried, the more gooselike it sounded.

Mr. Yee cleared his throat and dropped his baton hand to his side. Everyone stopped playing. "Let's try that again. Woodwinds, maybe a little less air?" he said, not looking at Shai. He was a nice person that way, not singling her out even though she'd been the only person in the woodwind section—the clarinets plus the flutes—to make a mistake.

Emmie Harper turned around in her seat; she sat up front with the other cellos. She gave Shai a big braces smile. She had just gotten braces, which she was not thrilled about, because she was no longer allowed to eat her favorite snack, nacho-cheese-flavored popcorn.

Shai waved to Emmie. Emmie waved back and made a goofy, wiggly-eyebrows face. Shai giggled; her bestie-best friend always knew how to cheer her up! Shai started to make a goofy face back, then stopped when she realized that Mr. Yee had raised his baton again.

"Let's take it from the top," he said. "From the top" was fancy music language for "from the beginning."

Shai made her face become very serious

as she resumed her clarinet-playing position. *Fingers, lips, chin, laser eyes.*

Mr. Yee's baton went up, then down. This time Shai hit the G note perfectly!

The orchestra continued with the piece, which was called "Opportunity." The piece was usually played by older musicians, but Mr. Yee had written a new, easier version. It was just the right level for the Sweet Auburn Student

Orchestra, which was made up of third, fourth, and fifth graders.

Shai, Emmie, and the other orchestra members attended the Sweet Auburn School for the Performing Arts. It was a school for kids who might want to become professional musicians, dancers, or actors someday. They took classes in music, dance, and drama, plus regular subjects like math, English, science,

history, and foreign languages. Mr. Yee was their music teacher as well as the boss of the orchestra.

Shai was most interested in the drama part of the school. She planned to be an actor— and also a veterinarian like her mom. And a dentist, too, because teeth were pretty much the coolest things ever. She liked dance and

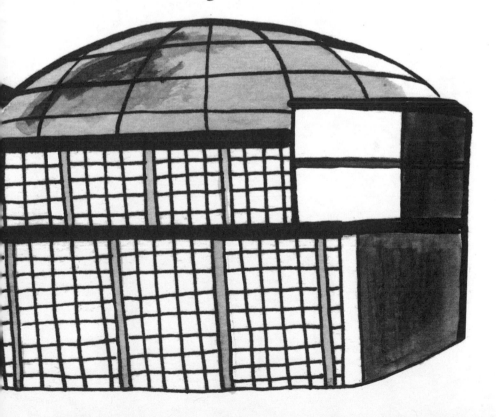

music, although she couldn't imagine herself as a professional dancer or clarinet player. But who knew? Her grandma Rosa liked to remind her that she was only eight, and she might change her mind a whole bunch of times before she was an adult!

A Concert for Animals

The orchestra rehearsal continued. First they practiced the beginning of "Opportunity" . . . then the middle . . . then the end.

Mr. Yee kept the tempo and beat steady with his baton. He used his free hand and the rest of his body to communicate different directions to different instruments. One minute he pointed to the violin section, clutched at his heart, and pretended to swoon; this meant he wanted the violins to sound lovey-dovey and

romantic. (*Ew,* thought Shai.) The next minute he pointed to the brass section while bobbing his head and bouncing up and down on his toes; this meant he wanted the saxophones, trumpets, and trombones to sound super-energetic.

The final part of the piece was even more super-energetic. As Shai played her notes, her fingers flying and her breath breathing, she pictured fireworks popping and crackling in the sky.

The piece finished with a loud cymbal crash from Jayden, who was a fourth grader and the percussionist for the orchestra. Jayden was Deaf, so she played in bare feet; that way she could feel the music vibrating through the wooden floors. She also paid double-extra attention to Mr. Yee's baton and other cues.

"Bravo! Brava!" Mr. Yee complimented the

orchestra. Those were fancy Italian words for "Hooray!" "I think this piece is almost ready for our concert," he added.

"What concert?" Shai whispered to Glenn, who was also a clarinetist.

Glenn shrugged.

Shai raised her hand. "What concert?" she asked Mr. Yee.

"Didn't I tell you guys already? I'm sorry. It must have slipped my mind!" Mr. Yee was not the best with details; his brain seemed to be always filled with great music and important thoughts. "This is our annual fund-raising concert. All the money we get from ticket sales will be donated to this year's cause, which is the Sweet Auburn Animal Haven."

Shai nodded excitedly. The Animal Haven was a shelter that took care of stray pets. Shai was a huge believer in helping strays. Her house was filled with formerly homeless dogs and cats that Momma had brought home from her veterinary clinic. Shai, Momma, and Shai's big

brother, Jamal, also volunteered at the Animal Haven one weekend each month.

Shai raised her hand again. "Can I be in charge, Mr. Yee?"

"In charge of what, Shai?"

"Well . . ." Shai thought it over. "Can I be in charge of posters for the concert? And maybe decorations, too? And the confessions . . . concessions—you know, snacks to sell?"

"That's very nice of you, Shai. Let me figure out what needs to be done and get back to you," said Mr. Yee.

When the bell rang, Shai put her clarinet into her case. The case had her whole entire name on it—Shaianne Rosa Williams—as well as some cool emoji and puppy stickers. Her head was already swirling with amazetastic ideas about the concert. Maybe they could put photos of adoptable pets on the posters? Maybe she could convince Grandma Rosa to make her famous blueberry muffins for the confessions—concessions—whatever—table?

With Shai's help the Sweet Auburn Student Orchestra was going to raise a billion zillion dollars for the animals!

Or something like that, anyway.

SCENE 3

Vitamin Food

"I have to go to Charleston for a week," Momma announced that night over dinner. "My friend Brookelynn is having a knee operation. I promised her I would help her with errands and meals and such while she recovers. My flight leaves this Saturday."

"I'll be Momma while you're gone!" five-year-old Samantha volunteered. "Jacobe can be my helper-person."

Jacobe was busy finger-painting on his high

chair tray with Daddy's homemade marinara sauce. At the mention of his name, he glanced up and draped a piece of spaghetti across his nose. "Kobee!" he exclaimed. He had just started saying his name, sort of.

"Buddy, let's get that spaghetti off your nose," Daddy said. "We *all* need to help out more while Momma's away," he told the four kids. "We can divide up the household chores."

"Can't Grandma Rosa do them? Or Aunt Mac-N-Cheese?" Jamal complained. He pushed his glasses up his nose; they were taped together on one side because he'd broken them during a basketball game. "My history paper's due next week, and I have a very important algebra test. There's also ball practice and coding club." (Shai remembered that "ball" was middle-school language for "basketball.")

"Sweetie, Grandma Rosa and Aunt Mac-N-Cheese have their own homes to take care of, and they have other things going on too," Momma pointed out. "They'll help out when they can. But Daddy and I are counting on you guys to pitch in."

Shai took a slice of garlic bread and passed the basket down the table. She tore off a small piece and slipped it to Sugar, her Morkie, under her chair. "I can be on pet duty," she offered. "I can feed them and fill their water bowls. I can walk the dogs. Jamal can change the kitty litter boxes, though, because, um, he's really good at that."

"Excuse me, what?" Jamal burst out.

"I can be the breakfast cooker too!" Sam piped up. "I know how to put the 'fidgerator waffles and pancakes in the microwaver machine!"

Under the table Sugar and Noodle the Poodle were wrestling and growling over the piece of garlic bread. One of the cats, Sweetiepie, took advantage of the situation and jumped onto the table. Then she hooked an entire bread slice with her claw. Before anyone could stop her, she jumped down and ran away triumphantly with the bread in her mouth.

"Sweetiepie!" Momma stood up to chase her, then sighed and sat back down. "I

really need to teach that cat better manners. Jacobe, honey, please stop pouring milk onto your spaghetti. Shai, you and Jamal can take turns with the litter boxes. Sam, you and I can practice with the microwave together, okay? Before I leave? And remember from last time how we can't put bubble gum in there?"

Daddy leaned over and put his arm around Momma. "Don't worry, Annemarie. We'll keep the place running as smooth as clockwork while you're away."

Momma smiled. "I know. I just feel bad leaving you guys."

Shai ate a forkful of carrots tossed with butter and fresh dill. Daddy had picked the carrots and dill from the vegetable garden; they tasted really yummy, like they'd come from a farm instead of the family's big-city backyard. Shai remembered that carrots had lots of vitamins, which were good for energy. With the fund-raising concert, and Momma going away, Shai would need a hunormous amount of vitamins to get everything done!

After dinner Shai helped Momma clear the table while Daddy took Jacobe and Sam upstairs to start bedtime and Jamal walked the dogs. As they loaded the dishwasher, Shai told Momma about the concert.

"How wonderful!" Momma said when Shai

had finished. "The Animal Haven will really appreciate the donations. They take care of so many strays."

"I'm going to be in charge of the posters and the decorations. And the snacks to sell too. Mr. Yee said I could."

"That's an awful lot of responsibility, sweetie. Are you sure you can handle all that *and* practicing your clarinet? And also your schoolwork and your chores?" asked Momma.

"Sure I can! I'm going to eat lots of vitamin food. Plus, I'm very extremely organized," Shai replied. "I'll make lots of to-do lists, just like you always do."

Momma laughed. "Sounds like a plan. Would you like a nice new notebook for your lists? I think I have an extra one somewhere."

"Yes, please!"

They continued talking as they finished with the dishes. When they were done, Shai went outside into the backyard to put the carrot tops and other vegetable scraps into the compost. A full moon shone brightly in the sky. A warm breeze tousled her hair. The tall buildings of downtown glittered in the distance.

Something moved behind the compost pile.

Shai did a double take. Had one of their pets escaped? Was it on the loose?

"Sugar?" she called out nervously. "Patches? Noodle? Sandy? Marti? Sweetiepie? Purrball? Furball?"

There was no reply. Shai peered behind the compost pile. All she saw were grass and leaves and twigs.

She then scanned the entire yard. There was the play set ... and the picnic table ... and the fort she and Jamal and Samantha had made

out of garage treasure . . . and the vegetable garden . . . and the just-flowers garden. But that was all.

I must have imagined it, she thought. She emptied the scraps into the compost pile and went back inside.

SCENE 4

Shai's Very Extremely Organized To-Do List

The next day during recess Shai sat on the spinning seat and opened the new notebook that Momma had given her. It was even nicer than her favorite turquoise notebook with the fairies and emoji stickers on it. This one was small but not too small. It was lavender and gold and had a picture of a peacock on the cover.

Best of all, the peacock's tail feathers were decorated with real gems!

Well, maybe they weren't real gems, exactly. But they might as well have been, they were so sparkly and litty-spagitty.

Shai spun around and around. The spinning always made her brain feel extra focused and smart. After a few minutes she stopped spinning. She pulled a pencil out of her pocket and began to write in the peacock notebook:

MY VERY EXTREMELY ORGANIZED TO-DO LIST!

FOR THE FUND-RAISING CONCERT

*Be in charge of posters!

*Be in charge of decorations!

*Be in charge of snacks to sell!

WHILE MOMMA IS AWAY

*Do more chores!

*Take care of the pets!

*Keep an eye on Sam and Jacobe!

Shai paused to think about that phrase, "keep an eye on." It didn't literally mean keeping your eye *on* something or someone. That would be weird. It meant watching something or someone closely . . . in this case, two someones who could get into trouble in a matter of seconds, like the time when they used peanut butter instead of glue to fix Samantha's toy fire truck.

Shai remembered a few other things to add to her list:

P.S.

*Eat lots of vitamin food!

*Practice the clarinet!

*Do homework!

Shai closed her peacock notebook and tapped her pencil against the cover. Nearby, a bunch of third graders were playing ballet freeze tag, which was like freeze tag except you had to do ballet steps when you weren't frozen. Among them were Rio, Ruby, Ben, Nya, Nick, Julia, Glenn, Jay, and Isabella ... and Gabby, who was Shai's frenemy. (Although, sometimes Gabby was more friend than enemy, and other times it was the opposite.) Over by the fence some of the older kids were trading cards, and others were playing backgammon and chess.

"*¡Hola!*"

Emmie skipped up to Shai. She sat down on the spinning seat next to Shai's.

"*¡Hola! ¿Está triste tu ropa interior?*" Shai asked. The two girls liked to practice their Spanish outside of class sometimes, especially when there was a quiz coming up. There was an adjectives quiz next Monday.

Emmie cracked up. "I think you just asked me if my underwear is sad."

Shai cracked up too. "Oops! I was trying to ask you if that's a new outfit."

"Ha-ha! 'New outfit' is '*ropa nueva.*' Or is it '*nuevo conjunto*'? Anyway, this top is kind of new, kind of old. It used to be my cousin Katie's, but she got too tall for it, so she gave it to me."

"It's pretty!"

Emmie's gaze fell onto the peacock

notebook. She ran her fingers across the cover. "Wow! Are those real jewels?"

"They might be! This is my new list-making notebook that Momma gave me."

"What kind of lists are you making?"
Shai showed her.
"That's a lot of stuff!" said Emmie.
"Well, I want to be super-helpful."

"Hey! I could *help* you be super-helpful."

"Really?"

"Really!"

For the rest of recess Shai and Emmie discussed and planned. They decided that Shai would come up with a list of snack ideas for the concessions table and then ask people's parents and grandparents (including Grandma Rosa) to make the snacks. Emmie would help with the posters and decorations because she was good at art; they could work together after school and on weekends. Emmie also offered to pitch in at the Williamses' house while Momma was away, even though she had a lot of pitching in to do at her own house with her twin brothers. (Her own momma worked long hours as a nurse at the hospital.)

As they talked, Shai made notes and sketches and doodles in her peacock notebook. She felt lighter and happier suddenly. It was definitely easier to be super-helpful with *two* super-helpers instead of just one. And it was definitely more fun when the other super-helper happened to be your bestie-best friend!

The Vegetable Garden Mystery

On Saturday morning the Williams household was more crazy-chaotic than usual as Momma got ready to leave on her trip to Charleston.

"Shai, please make sure to give Furball his ear medicine twice a day," Momma said as she double-checked her to-do list. Her suitcase lay open on the bedroom floor, with her clothes neatly folded and her shampoo and other bathroom things in a clear plastic bag. "He doesn't like it, so you have to distract him with a kitty treat."

Shai opened her peacock notebook and added an item to her own to-do list:

*Give Furball ear medicine twice a day! Use distraxion treats!

She erased "distraxion" and wrote in "distraction."

"Jamal, can you get yourself to your eye doctor's appointment on Monday at four o'clock?" Momma went on. "Grandma Rosa will meet you there a few minutes late because she has her dentist appointment at three on the other side of town. They can fix your glasses or order you new frames if they need to. Sam, don't let Jacobe play with your new Legos; he'll try to put them into his mouth. Also, no gymnastics on the bed, please!"

Samantha stopped in the middle of a somersault and pouted.

"Oh, and everyone? Aunt Mac-N-Cheese will come by when she can to help out, but she's very busy with rehearsals for her new play at the Little Theater," Momma continued. Aunt Mac-N-Cheese, whose real name was Aunt MacKenzie, was an actor—just like Shai, who intended to be a famous Hollywood actor someday, and just like Grandma Rosa, who used to be a famous stage actor when she lived in New York City. "She's also working extra shifts at the coffee shop next week, and . . . *Wait, where is my passport?*" Momma exclaimed, glancing around wildly.

Jacobe crawled out from under Momma's makeup table and handed the passport to her. He had put a shiny blue butterfly sticker on it. "Bubberfly," he explained.

Momma gave a sigh of relief. "Oh, whew. Jacobe, honey, that butterfly should probably live in your sticker book, okay?"

Daddy peered at his watch. "Annemarie,

we need to leave for the airport in fifteen minutes if we're going to make your flight. Kids, Grandma Rosa should be here any second. She's bringing sandwiches for your lunch, and she said something about the zoo later."

Samantha began jumping up and down on the bed. "The zoo! The zoo! Can I get Dippin' Dots at the zoo?"

"*May* I get Dippin' Dots at the zoo," Momma corrected her. "And no jumping! It's up to your grandmother. Also, that means no dessert after dinner."

"Maaay-be," Samantha said with a sly smile.

Actually Shai agreed with her little sister on that one. She had never understood their family's "only one dessert per day" rule. Desserts were the best!

Just then Purrball, Furball, and Sweetiepie

burst into the room, their paws thundering against the wood floors. It was hard to tell who was chasing whom. They trampled across Momma's open suitcase, scattering clothes this way and that. One of Momma's silk scarves landed on Purrball. The scarf fluttered from his neck like a superhero cape as he and the other two cats raced back into the hallway.

"*Cats!*" Momma yelled. "Purrball, come back with my scarf!"

"I'll get it, Momma," Shai said.

She rose to her feet and ran after the cats. They were practically flying down the stairs. When Shai finally reached them, they were in the kitchen fighting over a toy catnip mouse. Catnip was like dessert for cats.

The silk scarf lay crumpled on the floor. Shai bent over to pick it up; it smelled faintly of Momma's jasmine-and-honeysuckle perfume.

Something caught her eye through the window.

Outside, a creature was moving through the vegetable garden.

Shai pressed her face against the window, staring and staring. The creature was practically invisible in the dense veggie jungle. Was it a squirrel? Or a hunormous chipmunk? Or a runaway pet? She was curious to find out.

She folded Momma's scarf neatly and set it down on the counter. Then she opened the back door as quietly as possible and stepped outside.

Shai made laser eyes at the vegetable garden.

Carrot tops rustled. Spinach leaves stirred. Dill
and basil sprigs twitched. There was a flash of
brown fur . . . then white. She could barely see
it, but for some reason Shai had the feeling
that it might be a cat. On the other hand, she
didn't know of any brown-and-white cats in
the neighborhood, and besides, all the cats on
their block were indoor cats.

Shai squinched her face into a deep thinking expression. What if it was a *stray* cat? What
if it was homeless and hungry and didn't have
a warm, cozy bed to sleep in? The idea made
her extremely sad.

On the other hand, if it *was* a stray, then maybe her family could adopt it? Sure, they already had a houseful of pets. In the cat department they had Purrball, Furball, and Sweetie-pie. In the dog department they had Sugar, Patches, Noodle, Sandy, and Marti. And in the other-pets department they had the hamsters, Ham and Ster, and the goldfish, Goldilocks. Plus, Jamal had been asking for a pet snake because his bestie-best friend, Travis, had just gotten one.

Pets were a hunormous amount of work. Shai knew that. Still, what was one more? Besides, wasn't it her family's responsibility— their tradition, even—to help animals in need?

Shai saw another flash of brown and white behind the big, round cabbages. Determined, she got down on her hands and knees and crept

through the damp grass. "Here, kitty, kitty . . . or whoever you are," she called out in a friendly voice.

The brown-and-white creature startled and disappeared into the bushes. Shai jumped to her feet and ran after it. She peered into the bushes . . . and through them and behind them too.

But the creature was gone.

Now Shai had a new item to add to her to-do list:

*Rescue stray!

Tuna Delight

Shai sat cross-legged on her shiny turquoise bedspread with her Spanish workbook splayed across her lap. She had already changed into her favorite pj's, the ones with smiling clouds with mustaches, and was sipping a mug of hot cocoa with marshmallows, which was good for sleepifying. Across the room her favorite books were organized neatly, or sort of neatly, on the shelves: novels, detective mysteries, folktales, and true-fact nonfiction. On her desk her lava

lamp swirled and glowed and cast a spooky orangey-red light onto her dinosaur-tooth collection.

"'Red' is '*rojo*' or '*roja*,'" she said out loud. "'Orange' is '*naranja*.'"

Next to her, Sugar barked.

"'Dog' is '*perro*' or '*perra*,'" Shai told Sugar. "So I guess 'super-cute dog' must be '*perra súper linda*'?"

Sugar panted happily and curled into a contented ball.

Down the hall Samantha and Jacobe were asleep in their rooms, exhausted by a long afternoon at the zoo. Jamal and Daddy were watching TV. Grandma Rosa had gone back to her house, which was just around the corner from theirs. It was the house where she and Grandpa Lloyd had raised Momma, Aunt Mac-N-Cheese, and their brother, Milo. Shai still really, really infinity-missed Grandpa Lloyd, who had passed away when she was seven.

Shai thought about the brown-and-white stray in the vegetable garden. Was it a cat?

She wondered how to say "stray cat" in Spanish. She decided to look it up in her Spanish-English dictionary. *"Gato callojero,"* she read out loud.

Just then she had a brilliant idea. She would take a plate of cat food out to the vegetable garden. The *gato callojero* needed to eat, didn't it? Besides, if it ate the yucky, smelly, fishy cat food, that would mean it was definitely a cat— versus a dog or a guinea pig or a blue-tongued skink or some other animal.

Excited, Shai put on her fuzzy slippers and headed downstairs. Sugar followed at her heels. TV sounds and Daddy-and-Jamal-laughing sounds drifted from the living room.

Once in the kitchen, Shai got a can of Tuna Delight from the cabinet, opened it with a can opener, and dumped it onto a plate. Sweetiepie, Purrball, and Furball appeared mysteriously out of nowhere. They circled Shai's ankles and rubbed up against her, meowing and purring.

"Sorry, guys. It's not for you," said Shai.

The cats tried to follow her as she squeezed out the back door. She pattered across the yard in her slippers and set the plate down next to the vegetable garden.

The night air was cool. Shai peered around in the darkness. Mrs. Taylor next door still had her lights on. On the other side at the Wallises' house, their new baby was crying in a high-pitched, new-baby way that reminded Shai of when Jacobe was born.

"I brought you dinner, kitty!" Shai called out into the darkness.

The cat didn't appear.

"It's really, um, delicious!"

Shai crossed her fingers and toes, which was what she and Emmie did whenever they told a lie . . . and whenever they needed luck. In this case, it might be both.

The cat *still* didn't appear.

Shai waited and waited. She gazed up at the velvety black sky. She thought she could make out a constellation. It wasn't the Big Dipper or Orion the Hunter or Cygnus the Swan or any other constellation she recognized, though. Instead it looked almost like . . . a cat. Or could

it be a dog? Or a rabbit, even? Shai made pinchy fingers and stared through them with one eye closed. But still she couldn't identify the shape formed by the stars.

Five minutes went by, then ten, then twenty. Still no cat.

After a while Shai let out an exhausted yawn. The hot cocoa had sleepified her brain. It was time to go to bed.

"Enjoy your dinner, kitty!" she said to the bushes. And then she headed back inside.

SCENE 7

Is This Your Cat?

The Tuna Delight was gone the next morning. As Shai stood in the backyard gazing down at the lickety-clean plate, she was positively, definitely, 100 percent sure that the brown-and-white creature was a cat!

What next? Shai thought and thought. She probably should make positively, definitely, 100 percent sure that the brown-and-white creature wasn't someone's *missing* cat—maybe by passing out some flyers? And if it *wasn't* someone's missing cat, then she could try to convince Momma and Daddy to let their family adopt it?

Yes, that was it!

Now all she had to do was make some flyers.

Inside, Jamal sat at the kitchen table poring over one of his schoolbooks and punching numbers into a calculator. Samantha was standing in front of the microwave oven with her hands on her hips. She wore the same T-shirt she'd worn the day before; it was streaked with pink, yellow, and red Dippin' Dots stains.

"I am the breakfast cooker today. I'm cooking breakfast for everybody!" Samantha informed Shai.

"What are you making?" Shai asked curiously.

"Pancakes. They're gonna have strawberries

and whipped cream and never-ending rain-
bow sprinkles on them. And root beer, too!"

Root beer?

"Yum?" Shai said uncertainly. She bent
down and peered into the microwave. A box
of frozen pancakes sat unmoving on the round
glass tray.

"Sam? You have to take the pancakes out
and put them on a plate. And then you have
to hit the power button to turn the microwave on."

Samantha rolled her eyes. "I *know* that,
silly-billy Shai-Shai!"

On the other side of the kitchen, Jacobe
pushed a toy broom across the floor. "Kobee
keening!" he said eagerly.

"Good for you, Jacobe," Shai said, although
it seemed like he was just moving some
crumbs around. Still, it was nice that he was

trying to help out—and Samantha, too.

Shai grabbed a banana and a leftover corn muffin and headed back upstairs. She knew she had to get dressed for church soon. But first she wanted to make those flyers.

Up in her room she found some white drawing paper and markers. As she sorted through the colors, she realized she didn't actually know what the stray cat looked like. All she'd seen was a bit of brown-and-white fur.

But a cat was a cat, right?

She turned a piece of paper vertical, then horizontal, then vertical again. She sketched out a cat in pencil and traced over it with brown marker. She filled in with more brown but left a few white spots.

Underneath she wrote down their family's phone number and the words:

IS THIS YOUR CAT?

She made a dozen more of these. After church she would pass them out at the neighbors' houses up and down the street.

Either the cat's owner would claim the cat . . . or, if the cat didn't have an owner, the Williams family could adopt it.

It was a win-win!

SCENE 8

A Dramatic Discovery

On Monday during orchestra, Mr. Yee had the students run through their concert pieces. There were three of them in all: "Opportunity," plus a couple of pieces by two olden-day composers, Mr. Beethoven and Mr. Mozart.

Shai had a hard time with her parts, though. She kept messing up her notes. She'd been so busy with her stray cat project that she'd forgotten to practice her clarinet over the weekend. She'd been studying the clarinet for only a year, so it wasn't like she could coast; she still had a lot to learn just to get up to everyone else's level.

"Why don't we take it from the top? Good concentration, woodwinds! Now let's try for even *better* concentration," Mr. Yee said, not looking at Shai.

A couple of the other woodwinds—Glenn on clarinet and Julia on flute—did grumpy

faces at Shai. Shai felt her cheeks grow hot. Emmie turned around in her seat and made silent words. It looked like her mouth was saying: *Hi are you okay?*

Shai made silent words back: *Hi not really. I'll tell you later!*

She took a deep reset breath and assumed her clarinet-playing position. *Fingers, lips, chin, laser eyes.* She ordered herself to concentrate.

But it was super-hard. Her brain was wondering if the stray cat was okay. Shai hadn't actually *seen* it since Saturday. Her brain was also wondering if anyone would recognize the cat from her flyers. She'd left them on her neighbors' front porches yesterday afternoon, but so far no one had called to claim the kitty as their own.

Her brain was filled with other things too, like the fact that the fund-raising concert was in less than two weeks, and she hadn't even started on the posters or decorations or concessions snacks. Maybe Emmie could come over after school so they could at least make a few posters? Shai needed to catch up on her clarinet practice too—obviously.

Also, when was Momma coming home? Was it in five days or six? Even with Grandma Rosa's help, and with the whole family pitching in with chores, things were not going super-smoothly. At church yesterday Samantha had spilled a juice box all over her dress, and no one had remembered to pack a change of clothes. And just this morning Daddy couldn't find his cell phone; it turned out Jacobe had dropped it into the cats' water bowl and was stirring it around with a chopstick to make "soup."

After school Emmie got permission from her mom to go over to Shai's house. Daddy was home; he had taken the day off from his pizza restaurant to be with Jacobe and also to try to fix his soggy cell phone. Grandma Rosa often watched Jacobe while Daddy and Momma were at their jobs, but today she was in bed with a cold. Aunt Mac-N-Cheese had driven Samantha to her gymnastics class at Head Over Heels and was also meeting Jamal at his eye doctor's appointment instead of Grandma Rosa.

As Shai and Emmie searched for snacks in the kitchen, Shai explained about the stray cat project.

"Aww, poor kitty!" Emmie said sadly. "No wonder you're worried. What are you going to do?"

Shai told Emmie about the flyers she had passed around. "So far nobody's called. I think? Daddy, did anyone call about a cat?"

she yelled in the direction of the living room.

"Cat!" Jacobe yelled back.

Daddy appeared in the kitchen doorway. There was a butterfly sticker on his forehead. "What are you talking about, Shai? What cat?"

"Nothing! So nobody called?"

Daddy frowned. "Nobody called. What are you up to? Is there something I should know about, or—" He stopped and turned around at the sound of frantic barking. "Jacobe, Patches is not a pony! You get off her right this second, mister!" He hurried back to the living room.

Emmie gazed longingly at a box of microwave popcorn that was sitting on the counter. She reached up and touched her braces, which were purple today. "I'm not supposed to have crunchy foods or chewy foods or sticky foods or hard foods. It's so boring."

"Let's have grapes! Grapes are awesome. Plus, they're a vitamin food, and vitamins are good for energy. Does *your* family want to adopt a cat?" Shai asked.

"I wish! But Mommy's allergic to cats. And my dad's apartment doesn't allow pets. I know because I tried to adopt a dog once. Are you sure your kitty's still hanging around in your yard? You said you haven't seen it since Saturday, right? Maybe it went back to wherever it came from."

"Maybe?"

Shai rinsed grapes in the metal thingamabobber with the small holes in it like she had seen Momma do a billion zillion times. She dumped the grapes into a blue bowl and offered some to Emmie.

Munching on a grape, Emmie walked up to

the window and peered outside. "Um, Shai? I was wrong."

"What?"

"I think I see your cat!"

"What?"

Shai made a beeline for the window. She followed Emmie's gaze.

The brown-and-white kitty was back! It was in the vegetable garden, half-hidden behind the sugar pea plants.

Shai's eyes zeroed in on the plate of Tuna Delight that she had left out last night. It didn't look as though it had been touched.

Why wasn't the kitty eating the cat food? Was it having tummy troubles?

Ignoring the tuna, the cat moved out from behind the sugar peas and made its way toward the feathery carrot tops.

This was the clearest view Shai had ever had of the cat. She could see that it had long ears . . . and a white cotton-ball tail . . . and longish back legs.

"It's not a stray kitty. It's a stray *bunny*!" Shai exclaimed.

Shopping with Aunt Mac-N-Cheese

"Let's get you guys some of this nice cantaloupe melon, sweetpea," Aunt Mac-N-Cheese said as she pushed the grocery cart down the produce aisle. "And oooh, these peaches look yummy too!"

Shai and her aunt were shopping at Publix. Momma usually did the food shopping on Tuesdays, but she was still in Charleston. Daddy had his hands full with Jacobe and Sam and his pizza restaurant. Jamal was at basketball practice.

Grandma Rosa continued to be "under the weather," which was some sort of olden-day way of saying "sick," apparently.

That left Shai and Aunt Mac-N-Cheese to make sure the family had plenty to eat for the next few days.

Shai's gaze wandered to the shelves of green vegetables and fresh herbs that were just beyond the melon and peach section. Earlier today she had taken a book out of the school library called *How to Take Care of Your Pet Rabbit*. It had a chapter on the best bunny foods. Shai had written them down in her peacock notebook. Her family already had some of these best bunny foods in the vegetable garden, like carrot tops, dill, and basil. But they didn't have *all* of the best bunny foods.

Shai pulled her peacock notebook out of her backpack and flipped through the pages.

"Aunt Mac-N-Cheese, can we get some cilantro, whatever that is? And mustard greens? And water crest?" She tried to read her messy handwriting.

"You mean water*cress*? Are you making a recipe?"

"Um, sort of?"

"What sort of recipe?"

"Um . . ." Shai tried to improvise a reply. She had learned about improvising in her drama

BEST BUNNY FOODS

class at school; it meant making stuff up on the spot. "I'm going to cook cilantro and mustard greens and water crest soup for dinner tonight!" she said, secretly crossing her fingers and toes.

Aunt Mac-N-Cheese picked up a lemon, studied it, and put it into the cart. She cocked her head and smiled knowingly at Shai. "Sweet-pea, why do I get the feeling that you're not really going to cook a soup?"

Shai blinked. That was the problem with Aunt Mac-N-Cheese; she was an actor too and could tell when people were making stuff up.

Should I fess up? Shai wondered. So far the only other person who knew the truth about the stray bunny project was Emmie. Shai had *almost* told Daddy this morning when they'd run into Mrs. Tayler on the sidewalk. Mrs. Tayler had mentioned about the flyer and had said that the brown-and-white cat in the picture wasn't hers and had they found the owner yet? Daddy had made a confused face and said: "What are you talking about, Mrs. Tayler?" But Mrs. Tayler hadn't answered his question because she'd started speechifying about the high price of gourmet cat food and about how her Siamese, Mr. Graham Cracker, had escaped from the house on Saturday night and come back smelling like not-gourmet tuna fish.

Which explained why that plate had been lickety-clean on Sunday morning.

Aunt Mac-N-Cheese put her hands on Shai's shoulders. "Come on, sweetpea. You know you can talk to me about anything. So talk to me."

"O-okay."

Shai tucked her peacock notebook into her backpack. She took a deep courage breath. "I found a stray pet bunny in our backyard," she began. "I thought it was a cat at first, but it turned out it wasn't. *Anyway*. It's super-duper-shy, and it runs away every time I get close to it. But I'm not giving up! I'm going to catch it and find its owner. Or if it doesn't have an owner, which it probably doesn't, then I'm going to ask Momma and Daddy if we can adopt it."

"Oh my goodness!" Aunt Mac-N-Cheese gave Shai a big, squeezy hug. "What a kind girl you are. No wonder you wanted to buy all that salady stuff. Did you know that your momma and I had a pet bunny when we were kids? His name was Thumper, and he was a grumpy little guy. We loved him, though."

"Really? *Wow!*" Shai hesitated. "Is Thumper . . . is he still alive?"

"No. He lived to a nice old age, though. And he had a wonderful life! Your momma and

I used to make up silly songs to sing to him. We'd feed him timothy hay and kale and apple slices. And we'd construct these little houses for him out of cardboard boxes. Thumper really liked cardboard boxes because he could live in them *and* chew on them at the same time!"

Shai pondered this. Maybe she could construct a cardboard house for her stray bunny too?

"Your mom adored that rabbit. Between you and me, I bet you she'll say yes to adopting your stray bunny," Aunt Mac-N-Cheese confided.

"Really?" Shai said hopefully.

Aunt Mac-N-Cheese grinned. "Yup. Your momma's got a soft heart when it comes to animals—just like you. Come on, sweetpea. Let's go grab some cilantro and watercress and mustard greens!"

SCENE 10

Rescue Mission

The next night Shai and Emmie made a "bunny trap" and placed it at the edge of the vegetable garden.

The bunny trap was actually one of the Williams family's cat carriers with a long, sturdy piece of string attached to the door handle. Inside the carrier were the greens that Shai and Aunt Mac-N-Cheese had bought at the grocery store.

"How does it work?" Emmie asked curiously. She'd come over after dinner to help

make decorations for the fund-raising concert, and she'd offered to help with the bunny, too.

"We're going to hide under the picnic table, there," Shai said, pointing. "We'll wait for the bunny to hop inside. Once it does, we'll pull on the string"—she demonstrated, making the door clang shut—"and the bunny won't be able to escape. Easy-peasy, mission accomplished!"

"Cool!"

Shai had gotten the idea from a "cat trap" that Momma had improvised once to catch two very shy stray kittens that had been hanging around her veterinary clinic's parking lot. Those stray kittens had ended up becoming the marmalade twins, Purrball and Furball. If

the trap had worked for them, it would also work for the bunny, right?

Shai glanced at her smiley-face watch; it was almost eight o'clock. She motioned to Emmie, and the two girls assumed their positions under the picnic table.

They tried to stay quiet while they waited for the bunny to appear. Emmie moved her lips and did silent multiplication problems. Shai pulled her peacock notebook out of her pocket and clicked on her keychain flashlight to go over her to-do list.

Her to-do list had grown to about a mile long. Tonight she had math and English home-work to finish, plus half an hour (at least!) of clarinet practice. She'd also promised herself that she would brainstorm some snack and snack-maker ideas for the concert. *And* it was her turn to empty the dishwasher. *And* she had to give Furball his ear medicine, which had proved to be not fun because Furball hated the yucky-gloopy medicine, and Shai hadn't figured out how to distract him with treats because Furball was just too smart.

Shai tried to remember the last time she'd played video games or watched her favorite TV shows or just chilled on the couch with absolutely nothing to do or nowhere to be. It sure was a lot of work being super-helpful! Volunteering to do stuff for the concert . . . pitching in extra around the house . . . and now performing a complicated rescue mission to save a homeless bunny . . . she hadn't expected these activities to take up every spare minute of her free time.

At least she had her bestie-best friend by her side.

Rustle, rustle, rustle.

"Shai!" Emmie whispered. "Do you hear that?"

"Yes!" Shai whispered back. "Do you hear it too?"

"Yes!"

In the dim light the girls saw a small movement in the vegetable garden. They made themselves be ballet-freeze-tag frozen statues. They tried not to blink or even breathe.

A cloud passed across the moon. The darkness grew.

Shai and Emmie squinted to see.

It was the brown-and-white bunny!

The fluffy creature sniffed the air and hopped through the spinach and lettuce and squash. It nibbled on some basil and then some dill.

Emmie squeezed Shai's hand. Shai squeezed back and sent the bunny a magical mental telepathy message: *Go to the cat carrier, go to the cat carrier, go to the cat carrier.*

The bunny turned and hopped toward the carrot tops. Just then it seemed to sense the cilantro and mustard greens and watercress in the carrier. It sniffed the air some more and hopped toward the carrier.

Shai sent it another magical mental telepathy message: *Keep going! Just a few more inches!*

The bunny reached the opening of the

cat carrier and sniffed. It hopped inside—*way* inside, where Shai had put the leafy treats. She could barely make out its white cotton-ball tail.

Now!

Shai pulled on the string, and the metal door slammed shut.

Yessss!

"Here, take the string!" Shai shouted to Emmie.

Emmie took the string and wound it around and around her wrist so it wouldn't go slack. Shai hurried to the cat carrier.

Easy-peasy! Mission accomplished! Shai thought happily. They had rescued the bunny!

She knelt down in the grass in front of the carrier. She couldn't wait to finally meet the bunny. She couldn't wait to pet it. She couldn't wait to tell it that it would never, ever be homeless again.

She shut the latch on the metal door, for double-extra security, and peered eagerly through the bars.

The rabbit was cowering in the back and

shaking like crazy. Its big brown eyes were full of fear.

Shai's heart sank. Her happiness whooshed away. She hadn't expected this.

"It's okay, bunny! You're safe now," she whispered.

The rabbit kept cowering and shaking. It looked totally terrified.

"Shai? Is the bunny all right?" Emmie called out.

"I don't know. It's super-crazy-scared."

"Should I get more of those fancy grocery store vegetables for it?"

"Okay. Sure."

Emmie ran into the house. Shai bit her lip. All she'd wanted to do was *help* the bunny. But she seemed to have made the situation worse—*way* worse.

Her eyes filled with tears.

What was she going to do now?

SCENE 11

Momma's Wise Words

"Sweetie?"

Shai swiped at her eyes and turned around at the sound of the familiar voice. Her mother stood in the shadowy edge between the backyard and the driveway—clutching her suitcase, her silk scarf billowing in the evening breeze.

"Momma!"

Shai jumped to her feet and sprinted across the yard. She gave Momma a big, squeezy hug and breathed in her jasmine-and-honeysuckle

perfume. "I thought you weren't coming home till this weekend!" she exclaimed.

"Brookelynn's sister showed up in Charleston a few days earlier than she'd expected. So I changed my flight and took a taxicab from the airport. I wanted to surprise you guys. Is everyone inside?"

"Uh-huh. Daddy's putting Sam and Jacobe to bed, and Jamal's writing his history paper. Aunt Mac-N-Cheese is at her play rehearsal. Grandma Rosa's at her house; she's underneath the weather."

"You mean *under* the weather? Oh dear, is she okay?"

"She has a cold. She called today to check on us and said she's drinking lots of ginger-honey-lemon tea."

"That's good. I'll go by and visit her tomorrow." Momma gazed over Shai's shoulder at

the cat carrier sitting by the vegetable garden.
"Shai, sweetie? Why is that thing out here? Did
one of the cats get out?"

"N–no."

"And why is there a long string attached to
it? You didn't try to trap a stray cat, did you?"

"N–not exactly."

"What, then?"

Shai grabbed Momma's hand
and led her to the cat carrier.

She gave a quick explanation about the bunny rescue operation. She added that Emmie was in the kitchen, getting more veggies for the bunny.

"I promise I'll try to find its owner," Shai finished. "But I bet it doesn't have one, because I don't know anyone in the neighborhood who has a pet rabbit. Do you? Anyway, I think it might be a very excellent idea for us to adopt it. Puh-*lease*? Except . . ." She paused. "It's super-scared right now. You're a veterinarian. Can you fix it and make it un-scared?"

Momma opened her mouth to speak, but no words came out. She shook her head slowly.

Uh-oh.

"Why are you shaking your head, Momma? Does that mean you can't un-scare the bunny? Or that we can't adopt it?"

"Neither. Sweetie, I know you meant well.

But you can't just trap animals you don't know. What if it's dangerous?"

"How can it be dangerous? It's just a cute little fluffy bunny!"

"Let me see."

Momma sat down on the grass in front of the cat carrier. She craned her neck and peeked inside.

Shai tugged on Momma's sleeve. "Well? Can you un-scare it?"

Momma stood up. She stroked Shai's hair, like she used to do when Shai was Sam's age.

"Honey, this isn't a domesticated rabbit. There *is* a big problem with folks adopting rabbits and then changing their minds and releasing them outside, which is absolutely the wrong thing to do. But this rabbit isn't one of those. It's a *wild* rabbit. It's meant to live outside."

A wild rabbit?

"But we're in the city. How can there be wild rabbits here?" Shai pointed out.

"Wild rabbits live everywhere—in the country, in the city. No wonder this poor little thing is so terrified. Wild rabbits have powerful survival instincts; they're always on the lookout for predators. This rabbit thinks you're a predator."

Shai gasped. "A predator? You mean like a T-rex? *Me?* But I rescued it!"

"It doesn't need rescuing, Shai. It needs to stay in its natural environment. In fact, we have to release it right away before it dies of fright."

"Dies of fright?"

Now Shai *really* wanted to cry.

"I was just trying to help it! I thought it needed a home!"

Momma stroked Shai's hair some more.

"I know, honey. Your desire to be helpful is a wonderful quality. But sometimes help isn't necessary. And it can even be harmful. The best way we can help this bunny is to let it go."

Tears flowed down Shai's cheeks. Deep down, she knew that Momma was right.

She wished so much that Momma *wasn't* right, though. She wished she could keep the bunny and name it Thumper Two. She wished she could build it cardboard box houses for it to chew up. She wished she could feed it timothy hay and kale and apple slices and other yummy bunny foods.

Emmie came out of the house holding bunches of cilantro and mustard greens and watercress. Her worried gaze bounced between Shai and Momma.

"Hi, Ms. Williams. Why is Shai crying? Shai, why are you crying?"

Sniffling, Shai repeated what Momma had told her.

"Oh." Emmie rushed up to Shai and hugged her. "I'm really, really sorry."

"I know. Me too. But Momma's right."

Shai wiped her tears away. Then she bent down and unlatched the metal door of the cat carrier.

She, Emmie, and Momma stepped back and waited.

Five minutes passed, then ten, then twenty. The bunny poked its nose out and sniffed. Then it hopped out of the carrier and darted for the bushes.

"Good luck to you, wild bunny!" Emmie called out.

"We love you!" Shai added.

Momma wrapped her arms around both girls. "Let's go inside and make ourselves some

hot chocolate with marshmallows. Oh, and, Shai, sweetie? Did I mention I was looking over the Animal Haven website the other day? Do you know they have a new bunny available for adoption?"

Shai's face lit up. "Really?"

"I thought we might meet him the next time we're there for volunteer duty."

"*Yes!*"

Maybe Shai could give a home to a homeless bunny after all.

SCENE 12

Bravo! Brava! Bunny!

Mr. Yee scanned the faces of the orchestra. He nodded and smiled. Then he breathed in quickly and raised the baton.

Shai sat up very straight and made double-extra sure of her clarinet-playing position. *Fingers, lips, chin, laser eyes.* Her new concert dress felt stiff and crinkly against her skin. But she ignored the sensation and focused entirely on the piece they were about to perform for the audience.

A second later Mr. Yee breathed out quickly and lowered the baton.

Shai hit a perfect G—no goose honking this time! The rest of the orchestra hit their notes too. The music flowed and danced through the packed auditorium.

She knew that her family was sitting in the tenth row: Momma, Daddy, Jamal, Samantha, Jacobe, Aunt Mac-N-Cheese, Grandma Rosa, and also Grandma Marie and Grandpa Ben, who were visiting from Florida. Momma had also invited the entire staff of her veterinary clinic. Daddy's employees from the pizza restaurant were there too, and also Aunt Mac-N-Cheese's actor friends and Grandma Rosa's book club. Everyone was excited about raising money for stray animals!

In the past week and a half since Shai had set the wild bunny free, she'd been able to turn her full attention back to her mile-long to-do list. Emmie had helped her create some cool posters to advertise the concert. Shai had recruited a bunch of parents and grandparents to make cookies, brownies, muffins, popcorn balls, and other goodies for the concessions table, with all the money from those sales going to the Sweet Auburn Animal Haven too.

The musical piece flowed on. Mr. Yee kept the tempo steady with his baton. Shai had been practicing really hard to improve her tempo-following. It meant watching Mr. Yee's baton, reading her sheet music, and counting silently to herself all at the same time: *1 and 2 and 3 and, 1 and 2 and 3 and, 1 and 2 and 3 and* . . . She also tapped her feet for extra tempo-following purposes, although she did this in a super-stealthy, super-silent way so as not to distract her fellow musicians or the audience members.

The music reached the lovey-dovey, romantic part. Mr. Yee pointed to the violin section, clutched at his heart, and pretended to swoon. (*Ew,* thought Shai for the billion zillionth time.) Then he pointed to the brass section, bobbed his head, and bounced up and down on his toes. The saxophones, trumpets, and trombones responded by revving into hyper-energetic mode.

Then came the final part. Shai's fingers flew and her breath breathed as she played the fast, exciting passages. At the very end the percussionist, Jayden, came in at the exact right beat with her loud cymbal crash.

The audience burst into wild applause. Mr. Yee turned around and bowed. He pointed to the different sections to stand up and take bows too. First the strings—the violins, violas, basses, and cellos. Shai gave Emmie a double thumbs-up. After them he pointed to brass and percussion.

Then it was time for the woodwinds to stand up! Shai gathered her stiff, crinkly concert dress around her knees and rose to her feet. She heard cries of "Bravo!" and "Brava!" from the audience. She thought she might have heard Samantha shout: "That's my big sister! That's Shai-Shai!"

Afterward there was a short intermission. Then came the pieces by Mr. Beethoven and Mr. Mozart. And then came more applause and more bowing. When the concert was over, everyone gathered in the lobby for hellos and congratulations.

In the lobby Shai admired the animal-themed decorations that she and Emmie had put together. They'd folded cats, birds, bunnies, and other pets out of pretty origami paper. They'd

created a huge banner that said: THANK YOU FOR HELPING STRAY ANIMALS! They'd made posters with pictures of the pets currently up for adoption at the Animal Haven.

There *wasn't* a picture on the wall of a white bunny with light brown spots and big, floppy ears, though. His owner, Mrs. Grey, had taken him to the shelter because she was moving to a retirement home that didn't allow pets. Shai, Momma, and Jamal had met the bunny last weekend when they'd gone to the shelter to volunteer. Shai had fallen in love with him, and Momma had asked the shelter to put a "hold" on him while their family discussed whether or not to adopt him.

Emmie wove through the crowd and came up to Shai. The two girls hugged.

THANK YOU FOR HELP

"That was an amaze-tastic concert!" Emmie said.

"Amazetastic," Shai agreed.

Momma put her arms around both girls. "You know the best part, ladies? I just spoke to the director of the Animal Haven, and she said this concert raised more than two thousand dollars for the animals!"

"Yay!" Emmie shouted.

"Yay!" Shai shouted too. Two thousand dollars was a hunormous amount of money!

Aunt Mac-N-Cheese joined them and handed Shai and Emmie bouquets of daisies. "You girls were wonderful!" she gushed. "Hey,

G STRAY ANIMALS!

sweetpea? Tell me about that black-and-white kitten on the poster over there," she said, pointing.

"Aunt Mac-N-Cheese! You want to adopt a cat?" Shai asked, surprised. "You always said

your apartment was way too small for a pet."

"Yes, well . . . I'm sure I can make some space for a tiny new roommate," Aunt Mac-N-Cheese said with a wink. "And guess what? I just talked to Mom, and she might be interested in adopting a cat too . . . that old gray fellow on the poster in the corner."

"Seriously? Grandma Rosa's always complaining about the pets in our house and how much work they are!"

Aunt Mac-N-Cheese laughed. "Well, she'll keep complaining, I'm sure! But I think your lovely concert has shifted her mind a bit about how important it is to give stray animals a forever home."

"Golly, really?"

At that moment Shai was so happy that she could actually *feel* her heart growing bigger in her chest. She hadn't been able to help the wild bunny, but it turned out that it hadn't needed her help. On the other hand, she had helped raise a lot of money for the Animal Haven shelter . . . and had helped make her aunt and grandma and others want to open their homes and hearts to stray pets.

Best of all, Momma and Daddy had agreed that the family could adopt the white-and-brown bunny with the floppy ears! Samantha had already picked out a name for him: Floppy Ears. But Shai was hoping to call him Thumper Two, after Momma and Aunt Mac-N-Cheese's Thumper.

Or maybe the bunny would have a very long name: Thumper Two Floppy Ears Williams.

"Time for some celebration cookies?" Emmie asked.

"Time for some celebration cookies," Shai agreed.

The bestie-best friends hooked arms and skipped toward the concessions table.

Dear Readers,

I am so glad that I have this opportunity to share my feelings and concerns about the unfortunate amount of stray pets and what you can do to help.

I love animals and it is very depressing to see so many stray pets. I would like to save them all, but realistically I can't. I volunteer at my local shelter, participating in the Dog Socialization and R&R (Rest & Relaxation) programs. I have joined a club at school that focuses on the strays in our area. I also donate as often as I can.

Here is where you come in. We can team up to save as many as we can. You may ask how you can you help.

Here are ten things you can do:

1. Volunteer at your nearest animal shelter.

2. Help those stray pets you see.

3. Ask your family to help you foster.

4. Donate money, food, or supplies to animal rescue programs

5. Educate your family and friends.

6. Raise money for animal rescue organizations.

7. Create or join a club at school.

8. Adopt from an animal shelter.

9. Foster from an animal shelter.

10. Get involved, speak out, and spread the word.

Okay, peeps, let's go out into the world and make a difference!

Yours truly,

Quvenzhané Wallis